Temple of the Ini-ni-ni

Isndlanegou Path

Suessdee Tribe

Carefull Foot Crossing

The Great Rock

The Wet Land

Slithering Grasslands

NO LONGER
PROPERTY OF PPLD

Owatti gooseyem

Old Worn Path

Ant Mountain

MauMau's Haunt

Skyproweloo road

Cannibal Cove Village

Swigglewoo People

To my son, Dash — courageously live and let love always lead

In the village next to where the Ting Tang River falls lived a boy. His name was JuJo, and what he wanted, more than anything, was to go on the hunt with his father and the other tribesmen. But he was too young.

When JuJo complained, his father would smile and say, "Have patience, Son. The day will come."

But being patient wasn't easy. So JuJo made the most of his time. When he wasn't shooting arrows or tracking the trail of a bullaboo bug, he was right by his father's side, learning the little things in life that count for a lot.

Then one day the Chief called for him.

"Welcome, JuJo," said the Chief. "I understand you wish to walk with the men of our tribe."

JuJo bowed low. "More than anything!"

"Then we must test you to see if you are ready. At dawn tomorrow you are to leave us and head out alone.

"Take the path till you arrive at the Great Rock. You are to stay the night on this rock. Do not get off for anything. Return at first light — we'll then know whether you are worthy of being a tribesman."

JuJo gulped. He knew how dangerous the jungle was, but this is what he had been waiting for.

The next morning his father took him aside and said,
"Remember all I've taught you, Son."

JuJo waved goodbye and headed on his journey. As the path led him deeper and deeper into the jungle,

he felt smaller and smaller.

It was nightfall when he finally arrived at the Great Rock. Carefully, he climbed to the top and prepared himself for the night. The air was cool and carried with it sounds and stirrings of the restless animals. JuJo felt very alone and was grateful for the moon's light.

He pulled some food from his bag and was about to eat when he sensed something watching him. He squinted into the darkness . . . a twig snapped.

"Who's there?"

No one answered, but out of the darkness slithered a snake. It was as thick as the branches of the bongo tree and seemed to have no end. It coiled its body at the base of the rock . . . then spoke.

"Greetingssss!

I'm Samsoa. What'ssss your name?"

JuJo stood, trying to look brave, and answered. "JuJo."

"JuJo? A fine name for a sssstrong and brave young man . . . and here all alone!"

JuJo was flattered. "Thank you."

"And sssso wise, bringing food with you! I haven't eaten in daysssss."

"My father always says, 'Be prepared.'" Without another word, JuJo tore off a chunk of bread. "Please, Samsoa, have some. I have plenty."

"Sssso kind you are. But let's share our meal together. There's a lovely sssspot down here."

JuJo had heard tales of snakes all his life, not to trust them, but Samsoa seemed kind enough, and it was always a good thing to share.

"I'd be honored," JuJo said, and began to climb down the rock. Samsoa just waited, a smile spreading across his face.

JuJo was halfway down the rock when he remembered the words of the Chief. He stopped — and it was a good thing he did.

Samsoa had secretly been wriggling his tail to the back side of the rock where JuJo couldn't see. He was just waiting for the perfect moment to snag the boy — and then have him for his midnight meal.

When Samsoa saw that JuJo had stopped, he reached and grabbed hold of his ankle and squeezed. JuJo knew he had to act fast. Taking the bag from his shoulder, he swung it at the head of the snake. The whack sent Samsoa reeling; JuJo had just enough time to scramble up the rock to safety, dropping his food on the way.

"You're faster than I thought," said Samsoa. Then, seeing JuJo's spilled food, he gulped it down in one mouthful. "But ssssso generous!" he said as he slithered away.

JuJo knew he had made a huge mistake. He sank onto the rock, shaking with fright. He felt very hungry and very alone.

He was tired and wanted to sleep — until he saw a shadow move. He got out his bow and shouted, "Don't come any closer!"

But the shadow did come closer.

When it stepped into the moonlight, JuJo could see it was a big cat with padded paws and a snaggletooth.

"Hello, I'm MaShaku. Don't be afraid. I'm as friendly as they come," he prrrrr'd.

"I'm not taking any chances," said JuJo, who had learned his lesson.

"I understand. This is no place for a young boy. Why, you're just a tasty snack to many creatures in the jungle. It's a good thing I came along when I did. I'll take care of you."

"Thank you, MaShaku. That's kind of you." JuJo lowered his bow.

"Now tell me, why *are* you here?"

JuJo liked the cat; he seemed friendly and good-natured. So he began to tell his story.

"That snake! I could have told you not to trust him. You must be terribly hungry. Come back to my den. I have a warm feast waiting."

JuJo's stomach begged him to go. "Thank you again, MaShaku, but the Chief told me not to leave the rock — *for anything.*"

MaShaku thought for a moment. "My friend, I can't leave you here all alone. I'll stay with you for the night. You *need* company, and company is what *I* have to give!"

"Thanks, MaShaku, but I *will* be fine."

"Prrrrrrrrrrrrrrr. Move over, friend, and make room for me. I'm coming up!"

JuJo enjoyed talking with MaShaku while on the rock, but being any closer to that snaggletooth was more than he wanted. "MaShaku, wait!"

But the cat wasn't waiting for anything — he crouched, then leaped up the rock.

JuJo grabbed his bow. "MaShaku, no!"

The cat acted as though he didn't
hear; he just clawed closer and closer. Just
a bit more and he'd be on the top with JuJo.

"Don't make me —" said JuJo as he notched an arrow.

The cat stopped clawing and looked up. "You wouldn't," said
MaShaku. But he saw the look in JuJo's eyes and let go. He slid
down the rock.

Staring up at the boy, he growled. "Next time you won't be
so lucky."

"Get out of here, cat!"

"Prrrrrrrrrrrrrr. We'll meet again, JuJo . . . We'll meet
again."

MaShaku disappeared into the night.

JuJo then realized that MaShaku, though appearing friendly at first, was probably planning to have him for his next feast. JuJo let out a deep sigh of relief. He remained watchful, but as the night wore on, his eyes grew heavy.

Sometime later, JuJo thought he saw the treetops swaying, but there was no wind. He was suddenly very alert. The earth began to tremble. JuJo's heart beat wildly; something enormous was headed toward him. But then it stopped. . . .

"*Get off my rock!*"

JuJo was frozen with fear.

"Did you not hear me? Get off my rock!"

Into the moonlight barreled a beast, angry, wild, and frighteningly big. There was no mistaking who it was.

Every child in the tribe had heard tales of the Jungle King: Koka Maroka.

JuJo knew he couldn't fight. His arrows would be useless against such a beast. What could he do? He was terrified. Then he remembered who he was. He was his father's son. He thought quickly, and stood slowly.

When JuJo spoke, his voice shook. "King Koka Maroka, it's an honor to meet you. You are a legend among my people. We've heard you are the mightiest creature in all the jungle and the most feared. Some say you show no mercy and have no heart. But I believe they are wrong. I believe one who is so powerful must also be kind and generous and . . ."

"Enough!" the gorilla shouted. "Do you know that I can crush you with one fist? You have some nerve coming into my jungle, sitting on my rock, and trying to play games with me! What is your name?"

JuJo stepped back, hoping he hadn't made a foolish mistake . . . but he answered. "JuJo, sir."

Then Koka Maroka leaned in and whispered, "Well, JuJo, I must say I'm impressed. Never in all my years have I seen so much courage in one so young. Enjoy my rock tonight. And tomorrow, go tell your people what happened when you came face-to-face with the king who has no heart."

JuJo bowed low. "Thank you! You are a good king!"

The mighty beast grunted one last time, then turned and left,
just as he came . . . making the earth tremble.

JuJo could hardly believe what had just happened. He knew the village people would never believe his night's adventure. As he stood and stared, morning light spread across the jungle. It was time to go home.

Looking around one last time, JuJo saw something that startled him more than anything he had seen all night.

In the shadows of the brush, just feet away from where he'd been, was his father. Smiling widely, he stepped toward JuJo.

Then JuJo heard a loud cheer.
He stepped back and saw, in the trees
surrounding the rock, all the tribesmen,
each with spear at the ready. They
had been with him the whole night.

His father said, "JuJo, you showed true
courage and wisdom. You honored not only
me but the entire tribe. Last night you
proved yourself worthy to walk with
men. Tonight we will celebrate!"

The tribesmen cheered again and continued to cheer, in the way the Ting Tang people do, all the way back to the village.

Toksalot Mountain

Booga Looda Lake

MaShaku's Lair

The Land of

Ting-Tang River

Hoo Toot Mountains

Village of the Ting-Tang

Oopsiedaesi Gorge

Hydavae Village

Tinkatoo Pathway

JuJo: The Youngest Tribesman

Copyright © 2007 Mark Ludy. All rights reserved. Published in the United States by Green Pastures Publishing, Inc., Colorado. www.greenpbooks.com Written and illustrated by Mark Ludy Edited by Simone Kaplan Designed by Stephanie Bart-Horvath ISBN 978-0-9664276-5-3 Library of Congress Catalog Card Number: 2006911217 First Edition February 2007 Printed in Canada

10 9 8 7 6 5 4 3 2 1